You and Me

You and Me

Martine Kindermans

English text by Sasha Quinton

PHILOMEL BOOKS

All we need is you and me

to be as happy as can be.

And no matter where we go,

I will always love you so.

We could cross the world so wide

to see what's on the other side.

We could travel the sea's bright sands,

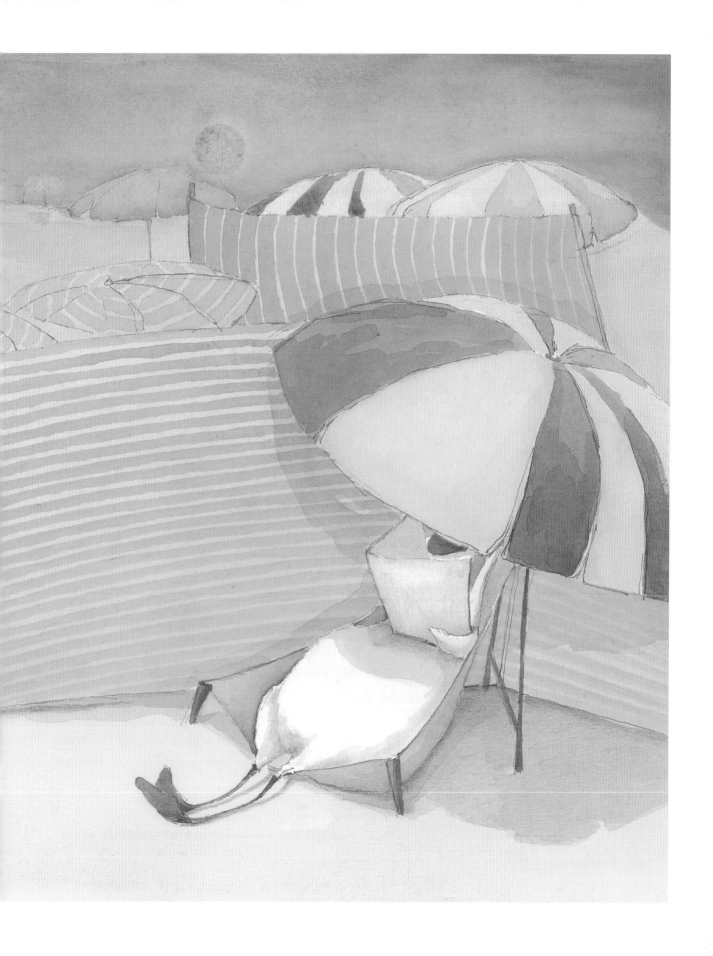

we could climb the highest lands,

or rest beneath the tallest tree,

still all we'd need is you and me.

We could lie upon the prairie grass,

or travel up a mountain's pass,

and no matter what we meet,

we'll always land upon our feet.

For we are dear and trusted friends,

and I will help you home again.

And on coming home you'd know

that no matter where we go,

all we need is you and me

to be as happy as can be.

PHILOMEL BOOKS

A division of Penguin Young Readers Group.
Published by The Penguin Group.
Penguin Group (USA) Inc., 375 Hudson Street, New York, NY 10014, U.S.A.
Penguin Group (Canada), 90 Eglinton Avenue East, Suite 700, Toronto, Ontario, Canada M4P 2Y3
(a division of Pearson Penguin Canada Inc.).
Penguin Books Ltd, 80 Strand, London WC2R 0RL, England.
Penguin Ireland, 25 St. Stephen's Green, Dublin 2, Ireland (a division of Penguin Books Ltd.).
Penguin Group (Australia), 250 Camberwell Road, Camberwell, Victoria 3124, Australia
(a division of Pearson Australia Group Pty Ltd).
Penguin Books India Pvt Ltd, 11 Community Centre, Panchsheel Park, New Delhi - 110 017, India.
Penguin Group (NZ), Cnr Airborne and Rosedale Roads, Albany, Auckland 1310, New Zealand
(a division of Pearson New Zealand Ltd).
Penguin Books (South Africa) (Pty) Ltd, 24 Sturdee Avenue, Rosebank, Johannesburg 2196, South Africa.
Penguin Books Ltd, Registered Offices: 80 Strand, London WC2R 0RL, England.

Design by Katrina Damkoehler. The illustrations are rendered in watercolor.
Library of Congress Cataloging-in-Publication Data
Kindermans, Martine.   [Du und ich. English]
You and me / Martine Kindermans ; English text by Sasha Quinton.—1st American ed.
p. cm.   Summary: A mother goose and her child may travel far and wide,
but they will always be fine just as long they are together.
[1. Mother and child—Fiction. 2. Geese—Fiction. 3. Stories in rhyme.] I. Quinton, Sasha. II. Title.
PZ8.3.K5654You 2006   [E]—dc22   2005014348

ISBN 0-399-24471-9
1 3 5 7 9 10 8 6 4 2
First American Edition